I0749401

MICRONOVELLINAS

and

PHILOSOBYTES

Rita Randazzo

Sprezzatura Books
South Burlington, Vermont

Sprezzatura Books

New Renaissance Press

8 Woodside Drive

South Burlington, VT 05403

ISBN: 9780970827982

Library of Congress Control Number: 2011963131

Author's photograph by Joe Randazzo

Our communication is getting shorter, simpler... Novels have given way to novellas, which will become novellinas, which will then become micronovellinas. At the next poetry or book excerpt reading, there will be only monosyllables uttered, and these will receive a standing ovation...

Rich Wedemeyer
from his blog, WikiDick's Place

Other books by Rita Randazzo:

The Country Kitchen Cookbook
Feeding Herself
A Passion for Flavor (with Eve Plociennik)
His/Hers: Mars & Venus Write Poetry
(with Joe Randazzo)
Fifty/50
A Haiku Diary

To Joe

for now, for ever,

wherever the wind shall blow us.

Worm Boy

The man thinks he is a worm. He looks in the mirror, and the mirror says "You worm." He supposes he should go crawl around under the dirt in the garden, but he has to get to work, so he ventures into the street. He dons the mask he keeps in his pocket, which is modeled on the people he sees milling about, and feels safer inside it.

It is a good mask! Nobody notices that he is a worm!

At the office, the mask stays in place well enough, though it's a bit of a job to keep it from tilting to the right. And of course the man has to avoid extended conversation or eye contact lest a co-worker discover his secret. He cultivates an aloof, slightly mysterious attitude that holds them at bay. He acts like he knows *their* secrets.

By quitting time he is tired out and has no energy to do anything but return home, where he can take the mask off and relax. What a relief. The worm in the mirror is the only one who knows him.

Lady Thanatoxic

She slides in under the door, or through a crack in the window frame.

She listens with blank expression to the jokes and joys around her, waiting for the good stuff: the scary lab results, the broken heart, the painful disappointment.

She smiles.

Soldier From the War Returning

He made of his home a battlefield. How else could it have been?

The History of Micronovellina

For sale, baby shoes, never worn.

Ernest Hemingway

I Wrote the Great American Novel

Why would anyone want to be a writer? It's an absurd profession, or avocation, or obsession, or whatever you want to call it.

Here are some of the problems it can lead to:

Lots of drinking.

Many hours staring at a blank screen.

Many more hours lying in bed with eyes open wide and brain ping-ponging around, bouncing off the words.

Keeping a pad and pen in the bathroom.

Incurring the wrath of family and friends who swear you put them in your story to showcase their warts. (You tell them the character was somebody from work, or somebody you saw on the subway, but they don't believe you. And they're right, of course. Writers are whores.)

Not to mention the depression that inevitably follows a huge campaign to find an agent or publisher that invariably results in a mailbox full of SASEs or inbox full of e-mails that say, *We currently have all the clients we need, you nobody.*

All so that when you go to a party you can say, when a new acquaintance asks what you do, instead of customer service for an insurance company, you can say, *I'm a writer.*

Whew

As a writer, you necessarily give away your secrets. Fortunately, no one is listening.

The Tao of Micronovellina

The story always was and always will be. It comes from nowhere, it comes from everywhere. It goes nowhere, it goes in circles. It is everything, it is nothing. It is only the story.

Namaste 2011

When I am logged in on Facebook
and you are logged in on Facebook
there is only one of us.

Is Writing a Religion?

Religion is that which is bigger than you are, and in which you believe despite all the dictates of common sense and evidence to the contrary.

First it shows you your sinful soul, then it forgives the sins.

Writing and religion have a lot in common: the willingness to embrace a practice that can seem nonsensical (Faith), the courage to go to dark places and do difficult work (Sacrifice), the experience of grace in the rituals of pen and paper (Sacrament), and the constant study of human nature (Scripture).

Perhaps writing is not only a religion, but writers its priests.

No Exorcist Needed

My soul is corrupt in the merely
ordinary way.

Genesis

That first night in the garden
when the sun went down,
the man and the woman did not know
it would rise again.
What a long night that must have been.

The Price

I'm not an –ist of any –ism, which is a free and lonely place to be.

I Wish I Knew Who Said This
(Please contact me!)

Religion, spirituality, however you define it—let's call it an alertness to another dimension of being that is not empirically provable—helps you connect more lovingly and fully to your family, your friends, and the world. A search for meaning must lead to a reaching out; if it doesn't, where does it leave you?

The Love of Micronovellina

It is a harsh and prickly embrace that will likely leave thorns in your flesh.

Vampyre

Love is red.

Not for valentines or strawberries,

but for fire and for blood,

for fang and talon.

Desire

Delirium

Destruction

Despair

Love is red.

Love

For Ever

Ever After

After All

All Over

Kisses

None for mister, none for missus,
No one wants your broken kisses.
Some too skinny, some too fat,
You can feed them to the cat.

Tell Me If You Know...

...how brown eyes can look so
cold sometimes, like frozen BBs.

The Golden Triangle

How his eyes gleam when he beholds it.

In the Bed

They tap at each other's bodies like
prisoners exchanging messages through
the cellblock wall.

In the Dark

They comfort each other in their humanness, broken by the journey into thin shards with sharp edges. They embrace the pain and caress the beloved's edges smooth.

Pillow Talk

Him: Well, I certainly wasn't Jiffy Pop
last night.

Her: No, you were definitely Jolly Time.

Marriage, As Explained to a Space Alien

Two people—usually, but not always,
one man and one woman—make a lot of
promises while under the influence of a
magic spell and then proceed to peck
each other to death.

Help Me Make It Through the Night

But then there's tomorrow night
and the next night
and every night after that
so maybe we'd better get married.

The Jilted Lover

With all the awful patience of a homeless cat
haunting the back door hoping for scraps
he followed her with his sad eyes
sure she would soon realize...

The Scent of Micronovellina

Fresh sea-air nose with a hint of rotting shellfish; top-notes of passionfruit, burned toast, and woodsmoke; tart mineral finish with a suggestion of Cuban cigar. Pairs well with urban angst and cautious optimism.

There's No Such Thing as a Synonym

Perfume
Bouquet
Fragrance
Aroma
Scent
Redolence
Pungency
Smell
Odor
Fug
Pong
Stink
Stench
Reek
Putridity

Four Perfumes

I like fashion magazines, all the clothes so
wild and unwearable, the models' hair
flying, the impossible shoes, but I can't
stand the fragrance samples. They all
smell the same, and they all make me gag.
I wonder if the mailman minds.

These are the perfumes I would invent, if
I knew how.

Apple Cider
Vanilla Bean
Fresh Bread
Sundried Bed Sheets

The Principle of Micronovellina

Punch ‘em and get out.

Fear of Flying

What do you call the feeling you have when you hate to travel?

Tripidation

Mother's Day

What do you call the best mother in the world?

Optimum

The Change

What do you call it when a middle-aged woman stops cooking?

Menupause

Dry Martini?

Absolut-ely!

Vrooom

Driving in the city in a car that goes zero to 60 in 4.5 seconds is like a woman who doesn't date wearing sexy underwear.

My Favorite Toast

Here's to being happy through intention, not circumstance, and to embracing the unknown loveliness.

A Six-Word Memoir

Blind date
sealed my fate:
Mate

Facebook Thanksgiving

TAKE THE THANKSGIVING CHALLENGE! Every day this month until Thanksgiving, think of one thing that you are thankful for & post it as your status. "Today I am thankful for..." Now if you think you can do it, then re-post this message as your status to invite others to take the challenge, then post what you are thankful for.
See More
November 9 at 8:16 am

Today I am thankful for, um, the alarm going off this morning so I won't be late for the dentist.

Today I am thankful for my husband, no matter how annoying he may be.
November 10 at 9:10 am

Today I am thankful for all who serve our country. I would like to thank the troops by bringing them home from wars we have no business waging! Hate that damn Dubya!
November 11 at 9:49 am

Today I am thankful to see the sun after so many cloudy, gloomy days. Burlington is the

cloudiest city in America, I bet. Can you spell S.A.D.?
November 12 at 9:00 am

Today I am thankful for breakfast. We baked Scottish oat bread yesterday, and what's left of it is this morning's toast. Delish, but soooo fattening.
November 13 at 8:32 am

Today I am thankful for my great kids. Without them I would be awfully lonely. Of course they're all so far away that I never see them. And they never call!
November 14 at 9:37 am

Today I'm thankful for the loving friends who enrich my life. You know who you are ☺ Don't you? Are you out there?
November 15 at 8:52 am

Today I am thankful for laughter. Classic comedies are good for that; last night we watched Monkey Business with Cary Grant and zeppelin-boobed Marilyn Monroe. A scream. It's lucky she didn't realize how stupid she looked.
November 16 at 9:20 am

Today I am thankful for thankfulness itself. I am learning that it can become a habit if practiced faithfully. I'm growing by leaps and bounds in my ability to see the brighter side!
November 17 at 9:50 am

Today I am thankful to have work I can do that stretches my mind and uses my hard-won skills. If only somebody would hire me.
November 18 at 10:14 am

Today I am thankful for a happy home. Except for last night, when he acted like a complete asshole.
November 19 at 10:17 am

Today I am thankful for the people who need me, even the ones who tend just a teeny bit to be users.
November 20 at 9:59 am

Today I am thankful that I had parents who loved me. Wish I'd known it at the time.
November 21 at 9:38 am

Today I'm thankful that two projects I've been working on are drawing to a close and a new one is waiting in the wings. Work is good! Paid work would be better!
Monday at 8:58 am

Today I am thankful for....a stove that works so I can keep churning out those meals?
Tuesday at 9:47 am

Today I am thankful for the silence of the house in which everybody is ignoring me.
Yesterday at 8:49 am

Today I am thankful for YOU, my family and friends, and for all my loved ones who are not on Facebook. HAPPY THANKSGIVING TO ALL! But why *aren't* you on Facebook? And why didn't you invite me to dinner for the holiday??

GLOOP: In Response to a Facebook Post About Gwyneth Paltrow

Joanie is taller than Tina.
Tina is smarter than Fran.
Fran is blonder than Sue.
Sue is a better cook than Mary.
Mary is a better parent than Pat.
Pat is thinner than Paulette.
Paulette is a better singer than Lynn.
Lynn is a better writer than Steph.
Steph is a better actor than Jan.
But Gwyneth blows them *all* to shit.

The Usual Hot Mess on the Red Carpet

(inspired by the Country Music Awards)

The fashion press
was not impressed.
They were distressed.
"She looks a mess!"
"Awful dress!"

Just Sayin'

Women are ruthless. No one knows why.
But it trumps sisterhood every time.

The Psychology of Micronovellina

Hilton Als writes in *The New Yorker* about "....the bereft sense that comes when a young woman throws her body away to satisfy men who haven't a clue why she might feel compelled to do so."

We are compelled to imagine her story.

Malady

She has no contagious diseases,
except for melancholy.

Just Remember, She Said...

...your disease wants you dead.

Mistake

He used to fear that he lived too much in his head, while others bustled about, talking and grinning. Then he realized that the others were also living in their heads. What looked like action was merely the enactment of a fantasy, which *truly* is living in your head. Think what mistakes dreamers make!

Dream Journal: Seven Entries

Cats: Often they talk and have human faces. More often they wrap their legs around my hand and arm and dig in their claws. I scream and am unable to get them off me.

Handbag: I lose it or leave it at home or have it stolen. I am panicked and desperately hoping it is only a dream.

Walking: Night streets, half familiar, ice underfoot or it's raining. People looking at me, meaning me harm. I become so tired I can't take another step, and then they.......

Bathrooms: I really need one and all I find is dirty toilets, floor awash with something best not thought about, soggy paper towels on the floor. The only usable facility is right in the middle of the room, no door.

Telephone: I am frantic to call home. I have no change, then I find some. But I can't remember the number. I phone the operator and she doesn't know it either.

Mountain: Climbing, climbing, rocks disintegrating underfoot as I go, destroying the return path. I reach the top and look hundreds of feet down into the abyss. Am I able to fly?

Parents: How I have been deceived! They're not dead!

Dream Journal: About My Sister

I had the most hilarious dream last night about a big crowd of people showing up in my basement for a party I had no idea I was giving. Among the guests were Oscar Wilde, George Clooney, Peter Haber, a guy named Glelly, a troupe of Israeli hora dancers, and you and Robin. She was a little girl, wearing a party dress, and you were dressed like Eliza Doolittle in the ball scene. You recognized Glelly right away (he was apparently famous, but I didn't know him) and said you had his book about Idaho. I was barefoot with dirty toenails, had no makeup on or a hair in place.

You were very thin and glamorous, and I asked you what your new diet was. You said, "I'm allergic to mid-nineteenth-century literature and find if I read a lot of it, I lose weight."

Dream Journal:
After Eating Too Much Pizza

She wanders down a city street and happens upon a fire sale in a fancy department store called Reefeee. Everything is priced at one dollar. Picking through the coats, she finds a beautiful soft gray wool with black velvet collar and cuffs, only slightly burned. The smoky smell goes well with the smoky color. When she gets to the cash register, the store owner throws in a matching hat. It looks like an upside-down black velvet salad bowl with a two-foot black plume exploding geyser-like from the crown. She is delighted with this hat and ties a spoon to it in case she gets hungry. Then she straps on her shoe skates and rolls off down the street, looking for her dog Frannie, who was also on skates and drawing a crowd with her jumps and spins.

I Just Ate a Vile Fishie By Accident!

Your disgusting anchovy pizza! I was wrapping the leftovers to put in the fridge and ate what I thought was a bit of sausage! But it wasn't!

Dream Journal:
This One Due to Meatballs

A white parakeet-type bird is hopping around the room smoking a cigarette with one side of his beak. In the other side is a tiny razor-sharp knife which the bird is using to poke holes in the furniture. My sister tells me gravely to be very wary of this bird because he is seriously evil. He can talk, and he hatches plots. He winds up in bed with me, and I lie awake all night in fear of the knife.

Help!

In the dream she is chased, again, and caught, again. But this time she is able to shout out the word, and it is heard, and she is saved.

The Murder Dream

She is rolled into a woolen blanket, lying on the living room rug in front of the woodstove, bleeding to death. No one can see that because the crimson blanket does not show bloodstains. In the morning, they will find a stiff red crust around an empty white body.

My Horoscope by Rob Brezsny 10/20/2010

CAPRICORN (Dec. 22-Jan. 19): *What is the wild and instinctual nature?* Radiance *magazine posed that question to storyteller Clarissa Pinkola Estes. Here's her reply: "to establish territory, to find one's pack, to be in one's body with certainty and pride regardless of the body's gifts and limitations, to speak and act in one's behalf, to be aware, alert, to draw on the innate feminine powers of intuition and sensing, to come into one's cycles, to find what one belongs to." I would love to see you specialize in these wild and instinctual arts in the coming weeks, Capricorn. According to my analysis of the astrological omens, you are ready to tap into the deeper reserves of your animal intelligence. Your body is primed to make you very smart about what you need and how to get what you need.*

Jose, Can You See?

For a little while, a couple of months maybe, my best friend dated Jose Feliciano, the singer and guitarist who much later had a big hit covering The Doors' "Light My Fire." We used to hang out in Greenwich Village, and Jose was playing at a coffeehouse called The Id. This was 1962, and he wasn't famous yet. He passed the hat for tips at The Id, along with another regular performer, Richie Havens, who billed himself as The Folk Swinger. Ritchie wasn't famous yet either.

My friend and I were 16. We didn't know anything, and neither of us had ever had a boyfriend. We wore our hair long and straight and had our sandals custom-made in the Village with our babysitting money. We were saving to have our ears pierced.

Jose was from Puerto Rico. He was blind. I have no idea how he came to notice (if that's the right word) my girlfriend, but he asked her to accompany him to a benefit concert he was giving midtown at a school for the blind. So of course she said yes. He was a musician, after all. She told her parents she was going someplace with me.

Jose was ambitious, and he had a manager named Hal Washington, who sometimes hired a limo to make it seem like Jose was somebody. My friend got to ride in the limo with them, but Hal didn't like her. She was distracting Jose from the big plans Hal had for him to make a lot of money. Jose wanted to make out with her in the limo, right in front of Hal, and she was uncomfortable but didn't know how to get out of it.

Jose invited her to visit his family's apartment on Second Avenue. His father and his many siblings all were blind or partially so. His parents said my friend could take Jose to the movies. He wanted to see West Side Story and needed somebody to tell him what was going on. She was nervous being responsible for him, having had no experience guiding a blind person, but he didn't have a dog so it was up to her.

She tried to explain about the Jets and the Sharks, but people hissed at her to stop talking and she stopped. All Jose was going to get was what he could hear, the dialogue and the songs. He liked the music. She guided him onto the subway and took him home.

Hal soon found a way to get rid of her. He told Jose she was flirting with the espresso guy at The Id, and Jose dumped her. Then Hal got him a Carnegie Hall concert, and she read in the paper that it was a smash. Jose even got to sing the national anthem at a major league baseball game.

The Benefit of Micronovellina

No need for a bookmark!

Livin' In the North Country

Blowing bubbles at thirty below,
they freeze aloft and
b   u   c
   o   n   e
on the snow.

Let's Hibernate

A mated pair
of furry bears
were living in a cave.

They wear what bears wear
(lots of hair)
and never have to shave.

Mumbly and Pumbly

The pair of bears
had a pair of heirs,
so they were a family.

The cubs were fat and the cubs were round,
one was black, the other brown,
and they sat on Daddy's knee.

Winter Solstice

The day grows so short that
drinking seems to take up most of it.

Passage

You are a snowflake that will melt
in the spring, as will I.

The Flavor of Micronovellina

It always tastes bitter,
because sweet is a lie.

My Face

Is there a woman anywhere,
in any country, in any culture,
of any time, of any race,
who does not as time passes
look in the mirror and say,
My face!
My face!

Vanity

She couldn't bear to wash the ugly body.

She felt her eyes blazing in her head, in
her vanilla-pudding face, suddenly
switched on like the high beams of a car
in the night.

She occasionally had a day when she
could stand herself, because she looked
okay. This mostly happened when she
took off her glasses before approaching
the mirror.

One day she became invisible to herself.
That was the best day of all.

I Was a Female Impersonator

Twelve years old, Mom gives her an "oil treatment" and sends her to the neighborhood beauty parlor for a haircut. Hair all gooey, wrapped in a scarf. Hairdresser doesn't want to deal with it and sends her home.

Twenty years old, working in Junior Sportswear in a Manhattan department store on 34th Street, the long-defunct Franklin Simon. Co-worker tells her she's a big girl and shouldn't wear those tiny ear studs. She loved them, before.

Thirty-four years old, walking home from work on North Winooski Avenue, a man approaching from the opposite direction suddenly grabs her arm and twists it behind her back. She slams him with her heavy purse, kicks him with her heavy boot, and frees her arm. What's the matter with you?! she screams. He yells back, What's the matter with *you*? Later her friend says, Well you do look pretty fierce, maybe he grabbed you 'cause you scared him.

Forty-six years old, gynecologist says she's beginning menopause. Can I still get pregnant? she asks. Better not, the doctor replies. Your eggs are no good now.

She also doesn't like chocolate.

At this point she thinks, maybe I'm not a girl at all.

What Bodies Are For

Children: running, skating, biking, throwing, getting dirty, skinning knees and elbows, crying, hugging Mommy, splashing in ponds and puddles, pitching sticks for the dog, playing team games on front lawns

Teens: playing team games on athletic fields, fighting acne, discovering, viewing in the mirror, strutting, trudging with head down, getting to first base, standing against the wall at prom, worrying, comparing, competing

Young adults: comparing, competing, adorning, preening, pleasuring, birthing, working out at the gym, relaxing at the spa, getting ahead, getting laid, getting promoted, going to Little League games, sipping cocktails

Middle-aged adults: sipping cocktails, worrying, viewing in the mirror, pinching an inch, writing checks, applying face cream, learning ballroom dancing, doing yoga, visiting colleges, fighting with their teens

Elders: fighting with their relatives, visiting the pharmacy, consulting multiple doctors, aching, squinting, going to church, playing bingo, paying medical bills, complaining, bearing up, being brave, praying, *remembering...*

Results of Deep Thinking Upon Turning 65

Aging is merely a matter of

More Deep Thinking

No one gets to keep their original packaging.

From Vogue to AARP

You know you're old when you are more excited that your blood pressure is down than upset that your weight is up.

Epitaph

When you are old,

When you are ugly,

When you are dying,

Will anybody know

Who you were?

What you did?

When you were somebody.

The Two Wolves

You know the story. Each of us has two wolves in our nature. One is evil and one is good. The one you feed is the one that grows strong.

The good wolf is: Peace
Joy
Kindness
Empathy
Generosity
Truth
Compassion
Patience
Gratitude
Love

The bad wolf is: Anger
Envy
Jealousy
Self-righteousness
Greed
Arrogance
Resentment
Lies
Fear
Hatred

Which wolf are you feeding?

Oh, really?

The Architecture of Micronovellina

Involves hours of consideration on whether *Wolf* should have a capital or lowercase *W*.

The Difference Between a Nonsense Song and a Novelty Song (product of a tipsy dispute, which he won)

"Mairzy Doats" is a nonsense song.
"Three Little Fiddies (Iddy Biddy Poo)" is
a nonsense song.
"Flat Foot Floogie with the Floy-Floy" is a
nonsense song.

Because they all fracture the language
with imaginative words.

"Wooly Bully" is a novelty song.
"One-Eyed One-Horned Flying Purple
People Eater" is a novelty song.
"I'm a Yogi" is a novelty song.

Because they're merely stupid and have
no redeeming value whatsoever.

Said He, Upon Fetching Me a Nightcap

Any less would be an insult.
Any more would be a crime.

Those Old Apron Strings

Watch them in the kitchen
our mothers and we daughters
grandmothers with the girls
who became our mothers
on and on like a procession of circus elephants
each holding the tail of the one in front
the cooking women joined by their apron strings.
We step in line when our turn comes.

They cook with what they have
and teach the daughters to do the same
on and on like the story of the world
down the generations
across continents and centuries
women tied by their apron strings
keeping us alive with their cooking
their chicken pie and empanadas
goulash and samosas
sugared cookies and good rough bread.

The Grapefruit Diet

It was a pretty good diet as diets go. We got to eat a lot of meat and salad, and we were allowed to drink dry wine and spirits. Big plus! And of course, all that vitamin C was great for our health. But after dinner, after our one permitted cup of tea or coffee was gone, we felt the panic of knowing that not another bite or sip could pass our lips until breakfast tomorrow. All night visions of cupcakes danced through our heads, and we woke believing we had eaten them.

Veggie Porn

Sauté shallots in butter to dress the
steamed broccoli, emerald as shamrocks,
exciting as a gasp or a moan. Braise
onions and crimson bell peppers in olive
oil and garlic until velvety as a young
lover's skin and melting with passion.
Stuff baby bella mushrooms with creamy
spinach and shaved parmesan, salty as a
sharp nip at the throat. Roast carrots in
thyme-scented oil till they become sweet
as candy or a trembling mouth.

The Art of Micronovellina

Chisel away what is not the story.
That which is left is the story.

Nine Lives, Seven Veils

The man was in love with his cat. It must have been her self possession, the way she stretched, the way she waggled her shapely little fanny, her elaborate toilette of face-washing and ear-cleaning that mesmerized him. The amber eyes, blinking at him, seducing him. Her particular tastes: beef and liver yes, plain beef no. Chicken and salmon maybe, turkey absolutely not. He began to call her all the pet names he used to call his wife. Lovely Girl, Little Star, My Honey. His wife had named the cat Boots but his secret name for her was Salome.

He bought her baubles she rejected, bored before she even played with them properly. She would let him stroke her only occasionally, on her terms, and bit him if he did not please her. She would give a little chirrup and dash away, compelling him to follow. And when she reclined on his stomach in bed, kneading him with paws and purrs, his eyes rolled back in his head.

How gross a human female seemed to him now! It disgusted him to touch his wife's smooth flesh. It felt all wrong without a lush fur coat wrapped round it. And she had no subtlety, whining that he never talked to her, asking for attention without the means to compel it, casting sullen looks when disappointed. How badly she came off compared with this ethereal, transcendent little creature, Salome, the one who roamed the alleyways of his mind day and night.

One day his wife disappeared with the cat, leaving a note that read: She was supposed to be mine.

On Adopting a Cat

And so we begin the dance that all
creatures do when they desire each other.

Or when one desires the other.

Shall I love you?

Shall I love you more than you love me?

How shall we get on?

Shall you love me at all?

Shall I take you back where you came from?

Pets We Have Loved, Lost, Rescued, and Occasionally Destroyed

Snowball
Tippy
Ginger
Figaro
Butterscotch
Mabel
Little Bit
Sally
Annabelle
Isis
Gary
Kiki
Rosie
Shadow
Mella
Puddy
Penny

My next cat will be called Ravioli,
and I shall never forsake her.

The Stealth of Micronovellina

The Beautiful and the Damned, a recent book by Siddhartha Deb, explores "the new India," in which a computer engineer sneaks invisible "nanopoems" into the chips he designs. We are everywhere.

La Giaconda

Heavy white lids

Straight nose pinched at the tip

Comely cheeks pale and plump

Pregnant smile

We will never know

Contrive to Survive

Dodge the bullet.

Roll with the punch.

Read his eyes.

Count the change.

Refuse to lose.

Keep swimming.

Summer Situation:
New Neighbors from Eastern Europe

I wish the Poles
would keep their clothes
on.

.com

.net
.org
.info
.biz
.gov
.edu

ones and zeros streaking through the air
like a flock of demented birds

.dotty

How to Be Too PC

Call a deaf person "aurally disadvantaged."

Call a short person "vertically challenged."

Call the popular houseplant
a "Wandering Hebrew."

Very Short Story (from my inbox)

Man driving down road.
Woman driving up same road.
They pass each other.
Woman yells out window, PIG!
Man yells out window, BITCH!
Man rounds next curve.
Man crashes into a HUGE PIG in middle
of road and dies.

The Mysterious Slipper

Who has not wondered about Cinderella's glass slippers and why they didn't crack into pieces when she, however slender she might have been, stepped on them?

Perhaps they were not glass at all. The most famous version of the fairy tale was written in French, which renders "glass" as *verre*. But the pronunciation is exactly the same as *vair*, or "squirrel fur," and *vert*, "green."

Picture a storyteller narrating the tale of Cinderella around a campfire, telling about the fur slipper, or the green slipper, while some anonymous scribe mistranslates.

The Philosophy of Micronovellina

One word is worth a thousand pictures.

Butterflies

flutter by

Accessories After the Fact

• Photo Stories •

Washington Square Park

He played the lute. She was from Long Island.

M.I.A.

Missing.U.Awfully.

Lost on Lake Champlain

I asked my love to take a walk...

One-Night Stand

Looking for Mr. Goodbar

Finnegan

...a way a lone a last a loved a long the
riverrun, past Eve and Adam's...

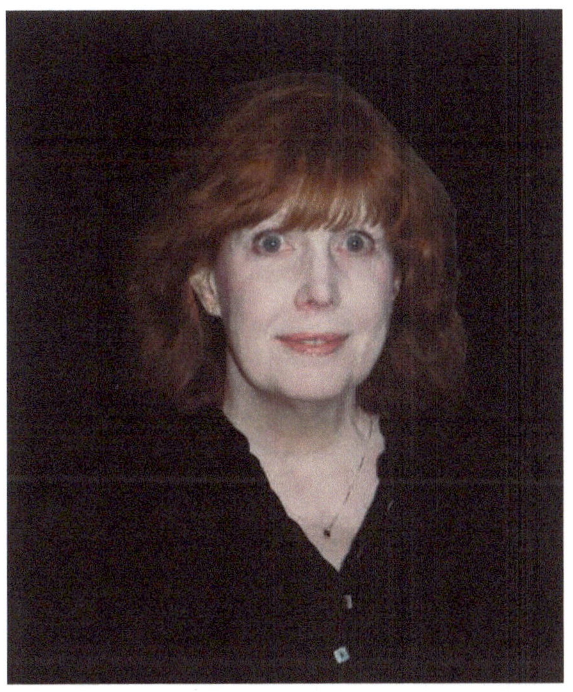

Rita Randazzo is the author of six previous books, four poetry collections and two cookbooks. She lives in Vermont with her husband Joe, where they grow tomatoes in the summer and chop firewood in winter.

www.ingramcontent.com/pod-product-compliance
Lightning Source LLC
Chambersburg PA
CBHW041407010726
47507CB00001B/28

* 9 7 8 0 9 7 0 8 2 7 9 8 2 *